It's OK

PAGE PUBLISHING, INC.
Conneaut Lake, PA

First originally published by Page Publishing 2021

ISBN 978-1-6624-3719-9 (pbk)
ISBN 978-1-6624-3720-5 (digital)

Printed in the United States of America

It's OK

Jayne Lively

It's OK, I say
to myself every day
when I get up in the morning
to start a new day.

Decide, decide what to wear.
I like that top with the little squares.
Do I wear my jeans that are faded blue?
Or my old worn-out pink tennis shoes?
I think I will wear what my mood is today.
If it doesn't match, that's OK.

Long hair, short hair,
black hair or blue,
the style you wear
should be up to you.

You may need glasses
to see far or near.
This is perfectly OK
as long as it's clear.

9

When you smile a big smile
and grin ear to ear,
some may need braces
to wear for a year.

One other feature that
no one can miss
are the shape of your lips
when you blow a big kiss.

Some people run fast,
and some people run slow.
It really doesn't matter
as long as you know.

It's OK to be first.
It's OK to be last.
It's OK to run
at the back of the pack.

When you walk down the street
or you look at the stars,
it's easy to see
how different we are.

If all fences were white
and all houses were blue,
all dogs were named Spot,
and all girls were named Sue.

If we all were the same
in everything we do,
I don't think I could tell
if it's me or you.

People can be judged by
what they say or do.
You need to remember
to let you be you!

About the Author

Jayne Lively has had this idea for a children's book in the back of her mind for several years. After thirty-eight years of working at a large corporation, she retired and finally pursued her dream of writing. With the loving support of her husband and best friend of forty-three years, she is making her dream a reality.

CPSIA information can be obtained
at www.ICGtesting.com
Printed in the USA
LVHW070624200721
693162LV00006B/147